— CONTINENTS —

SOUTH AMERICA

Erinn Banting

WEIGL PUBLISHERS INC.

Published by Weigl Publishers Inc.
350 5th Avenue, Suite 3304, PMB 6G
New York, NY 10118-0069 USA
Web site: www.weigl.com

Library of Congress Cataloging-in-Publication Data

Banting, Erinn.
South America / Erinn Banting.
p. cm. -- (Continents)
Includes index.
ISBN 1-59036-322-1 (hard cover : alk. paper) -- ISBN 1-59036-329-9 (soft cover : alk. paper)
1. South America--Juvenile literature. I. Title. II. Continents (New York, N.Y.)
F2208.5.B36 2006
980--dc22
2005003867

Printed in the United States of America
1 2 3 4 5 6 7 8 9 10 09 08 07 06 05

All of the Internet URLs given in the book were valid at the time of publication. However, due to the dynamic nature of the Internet, some addresses may have changed, or sites may have ceased to exist since publication. While the author and publisher regret any inconvenience this may cause readers, no responsibility for any such changes can be accepted by either the author or the publisher.

Project Coordinator
Heather C. Hudak

Copy Editor
Tina Schwartzenberger

Designer
Terry Paulhus

Layout
Gregg Muller
Kathryn Livingstone

Photo Researcher
Kim Winiski

Photograph Credits

Every reasonable effort has been made to trace ownership and to obtain permission to reprint copyright material. The publishers would be pleased to have any errors or omissions brought to their attention so that they may be corrected in subsequent printings.

Cover: Torres del Paine National Park in Chile covers 447,529 acres (181,000 hectares) of land. It is open to tourists and South Americans year round. (Getty Images/Photographer's Choice/Eduardo Garcia)

Credits: Getty Images: pages 1 (Photographer's Choice/Eduardo Garcia), 4–5 (Taxi), 6L (The Image Bank/JH Pete Carmichael), 6TR (Taxi/Luis Rosendo), 6BR (Brand X Pictures/Philip Coblentz), 8 (The Image Bank/Geoffrey Clifford), 9 (The Image Bank/Joseph Van Os), 10 (National Geographic/Joel Sartore), 11T (Andre Felipe), 11B (National Geographic/Joel Sartore), 12L (AFP/Vanderlei Almedia), 12R (Stone/Robert Frerck), 13T (National Geographic/Kenneth Garrett), 13B (National Geographic/Jason Edwards), 14L (Taxi/Eduardo Garcia), 14R (Stone/Aldo Brando), 15 (Time Life Pictures/Mirek Towski), 16 (Kean Collection), 17L (Henry Guttmann), 17R (Stock Montage), 18 (Hulton Archive), 19 (Time Life Pictures/Mansell), 20 (Taxi/Eduardo Garcia), 21 (Photodisc Green/Adalberto Rios Szalay/Sexto Sol), 22 (Digital Vision), 23L (Photographer's Choice/Donald Nausbaum), 23R (Oscar Sabetta), 24B (Stone/Glen Allison), 24T (Liason/Piero Pomponi), 25 (Alexander Tamargo), 26 (AFP/Rodrigo Arangua), 27T (Allsport/Mike Hewitt), 27B (AFP/Jean-Loup Gautreau), 28 (Taxi/Alan Kearney), 29T (National Geographic/Maria Stenzel), 29B (FoodPix/John E. Kelly), 31 (The Image Bank/Joseph Van Os).

— CONTINENTS —

SOUTH AMERICA

TABLE OF CONTENTS

Introduction

From tropical rain forests to frozen **glaciers**, South America has some of the most varied landscapes on Earth. Diverse wildlife and people also live on the continent. Animals, such as monkeys, jaguars, and parrots, leap, crawl, and fly through the mountains, deserts, and lush forests.

The original inhabitants of the continent, such as the **Inca**, lived in complex cities. The cities had large stone buildings connected by paved roads and bridges. Today, **historians** study the ruins of Inca civilizations, located high in the Andes Mountains. Many tourists also visit the ruins.

Spanish and Portuguese explorers arrived between the 1500s and 1700s and settled on lands belonging to the **indigenous** South Americans. They established settlements that formed the countries of South America. South America was named after Italian explorer Amerigo Vespucci, who landed on its shores in 1498.

South America is a large, cone-shaped continent. It stretches from a point above the **equator** to a tip called Cape Horn. Cape Horn is approximately 600 miles (966 kilometers) away from Antarctica, the coldest continent on Earth. A narrow stretch of land called the Isthmus of Panama connects the top of South America to North America.

Water surrounds South America. The Caribbean Sea is to the north, the Atlantic Ocean borders the east coast, and the Pacific Ocean borders the west coast. Large ships carrying people, tourists, and cargo dock at major ports along the continent's nearly 12,000 miles (19,312 km) of coast. Bolivia and Paraguay, in the center of the continent, are the only two South American countries that do not border an ocean.

The ruins of the ancient city of Machu Picchu stand in the mountains of south-central Peru. The city is about 600 years old.

South America

South America is the fourth-largest continent in the world. Asia, Africa, and North America are larger. The continent is divided into twelve countries: Argentina, Bolivia, Brazil, Chile, Colombia, Ecuador, Guyana, Paraguay, Peru, Suriname, Uruguay, and Venezuela. France, a country in Europe, owns French Guiana, a region located in northeastern South America. Brazil is South America's largest country. It covers nearly one-quarter of the continent's surface. Suriname is the smallest country. The most populated city in South America is São Paulo, Brazil.

More than 3,000 orchid species grow in Ecuador.

Fast Facts

Buenos Aires is the capital and largest city in Argentina. The city is Argentina's major trading center.

South America is home to the world's largest rain forest, the Amazon Rain Forest. It covers more than 2 million square miles (5 million square kilometers) and stretches from the Andes to Brazil.

South American Continent Map

Location and Resources

Land and Climate

South America stretches more than 6,880,500 square miles (17,819,000 sq km) of land. The Andes Mountains extend 4,500 miles (7,242 km) along the continent's western coast. These mountains are sometimes called the "backbone of South America" because they run along the entire coast, from Venezuela in the north to Cape Horn in the south.

South America has three main geographic regions. The Guiana and Brazilian Highlands make up the eastern region. This highland region is made up of ancient mountain ranges that wind and rain **eroded** over time. The Andes region includes the mountain range with the same name. The large region in the center of the continent is called the central plains. The plains are divided into five areas—the Ilanos, the Selvas, the Gran Chaco,

The Atacama Desert forms part of the South American shoreline.

the Pampas, and Patagonia. The Amazon, Orinoco, and Río de la Plata Rivers crisscross the land and provide water to the farms and forests that cover the plains.

South America's climate varies from the tropical regions in the north to the frozen landscapes in the south. Much of South America is located south of the equator. The area around the equator is the warmest land on Earth. As a result, the climate becomes cooler the farther south a person travels.

Earthquakes are a shaking or trembling of Earth's surface. They are caused by rock, lava, or hot gas moving deep inside Earth. Earthquakes are common in South America. In mountainous regions, earthquakes often cause landslides. During a landslide, earth, trees, and even people's homes slide down the sides of steep cliffs.

Fast Facts

Tierra del Fuego, which means "land of fire," is one the coldest places in South America. Spanish explorers named the island after seeing indigenous peoples' fires burning brightly on the shores.

The tallest peak in South America is Mount Aconcagua, in Argentina. The peak is 22,834 feet (6,960 meters) tall.

The Andes Mountains are filled with steep canyons and tall plateaus. A plateau is a large, flat area of land. Some plateaus are very large. The Altiplano Plateau in western Bolivia is the same size as the state of New York.

More than 50 peaks in the Andes Mountains are higher than 21,325 feet (6,500 m).

The Atacama Desert in Chile receives less rain than any other place in the world.

The Toco toucan is one of many birds that can be found in South America's Iguaçu Falls National Park.

Some high peaks in the Andes are covered in snow throughout the year.

Plants and Animals

South America is home to many diverse plants and animals. Hundreds of trees and plants, such as mahogany, palms, and bamboo, grow in tropical rain forests. These plants and trees form a canopy, or roof, over orchids and ferns that grow in the **fertile** soil below. In the drier regions of South America, such as Gran Chaco, tall grasses called savannahs or *campos* grow among carob trees. In the mountainous areas of the west, low bushes and grasses cling to the rocky sides of steep mountains. In the frozen south, near Cape Horn, and on the island of Tierra del Fuego, few plants grow because the temperatures are too low.

Many of the animals in South America do not live in any other place in the world. Guanacos and vicuñas, which are related to camels, roam through the Andes Mountains. Guinea pigs, which many people keep as pets in other parts of the world, live in the wild. The spectacled bear is the only bear species native to South America. It lives in mountainous regions.

Wolves and armadillos live on South America's central plains. Hundreds of ant species that live on the plains and in rain forests provide food for anteaters and antbirds. Marmosets are a type of monkey that live in South America's rain forests.

Black ear-tufted marmosets live in South America's tropical and subtropical forests. They run and hop through trees and bushes.

Fast Facts

Selva is the Spanish word for jungle. It is also the name of the part of South America that is covered by thick rain forests.

Sloths are large creatures that live in South America's rain forests. They spend most of their time hanging upside-down from tree branches. Sloths often eat upside down.

Bullet ants, which live in South America's rain forests, can grow 1 inch (2.5 centimeters) long.

Natural Resources

Bananas, coffee, chocolate, and nuts come from South America. Sugarcane and cotton also grow well in the tropical north. Corn and wheat grow well in the dry south. In the mountains of Chile and Argentina, people grow grapes that are made into world-famous wines.

South American coffee is sold around the world. Countries with warm climates and fertile soil, such as Brazil and Colombia, can easily grow the tasty beans. Cacao is also grown in South America and is **exported** to many countries. Cacao is used to make chocolate.

South America has a successful mining industry. In Bolivia and Peru, people dig for silver. Chile has many rich copper mines. Colombia has a wealth of gold and diamonds. Lumber from mahogany and cedar trees is also exported and used to make furniture.

Fast Facts

Most crops grown in South America are raised for individual families or local use. Corn is a staple product that is grown throughout the continent.

Logging in South America has destroyed many of its rain forests. This logging destroys the **habitats** of thousands of species of plants, animals, and insects.

Cattle raised on the Pampas are exported to countries around the world. The cattle are raised on large ranches and are herded by cowboys called *gauchos*.

Coal, petroleum, and natural gas are also important resources in South America.

The Chuquicamata Copper Refinery is one of the largest in the world. This facility can refine more than 1,874 tons (1,700 tonnes) of copper daily.

Economy

Tourism

South America's dangerous mountain peaks, miles of sandy beaches, fascinating historic sites, and exciting cities draw millions of tourists from around the world.

People flock to South America's major cities, such as São Paulo, Rio de Janeiro, and Buenos Aires, to see the sights and enjoy the warm weather. Tourists sample traditional South American dishes, such as *empanadas*, which are pastries filled with meat, vegetables, seafood, cheese, or fruit. Tourists can also listen to vibrant and fast-paced **salsa** music played by street performers or in cafés and restaurants. Many people also visit Brasília, the capital of Brazil. The city is shaped like an airplane. People take helicopter tours above the city to see the amazing sight.

Buenos Aires is known as the city where the tango originated.

Each year during Carnaval, a parade is held in Rio de Janeiro.

Natural wonders also draw tourists to South America. People raft down the winding Amazon River. In some places the river is calm. Many people enjoy seeing the plants, animals, and people that live along the river's coasts. In other places, the water is rough and flows quickly. Tourists seeking adventure take white-water rafting trips in these areas.

One of the most popular tourist destinations in South America is Machu Picchu. This historic site was discovered in 1911. At Machu Picchu, people tour through the ruins of an ancient Incan city. The ruins include old stone buildings and terraces, which were steps used to grow crops.

Chokepukio is an archaeological site located in the Valley of Cuzco, Peru. Wari Indian artifacts have been found at the site.

Fast Facts

The Iguaçu Falls in Argentina is the largest waterfall in South America. Tons of water pour over the waterfall, which is about 1 mile (1.6 km) wide.

Tierra del Fuego's unique climate and landscape attracts many visitors. Animals, such as penguins, which normally live in very cold climates, call Tierra del Fuego their home.

As many as 2,000 people visit Machu Picchu each day. The site earns Peru $6 million U.S. annually.

La Boca, a colorful neighborhood in Argentina, contains some of the oldest buildings in South America. It is a World Heritage Site, which means the area is protected from being destroyed.

Industry

South America's abundance of natural resources and breathtaking sights make agriculture, forestry, mining, and tourism the continent's largest industries.

Farms are scattered throughout South America. In drier regions, people grow potatoes, corn, and wheat. In the east, many South Americans work on coffee and cacao plantations, or large farms. Most coffee consumed around the world comes from South America. Brazil grows more coffee than any other country in the world.

The lumber industry is important in South America. Not all trees are used for their wood. The liquid in rubber trees is used to create tires, construction equipment, and clothing, such as rubber boots. Brazil nuts, which are actually long, thick seeds, get their name from the country where they grow. The seeds are salted and roasted in processing plants, and sent around the world for people to enjoy.

Reserves of precious metals and **minerals** drew early Spanish explorers to South America. Gold, silver, copper, and iron ore, which is used to make iron, are mined across the continent.

Fast Facts

When Christopher Columbus arrived in South America, he learned that the indigenous South Americans used rubber to make certain types of clothing, such as shoes and coats. Rubber was not widely used in Europe for nearly 200 years after Columbus's visit.

Most people who work in the lumber industry live in cities and towns along the Amazon River. The river is used to transport large loads of wood from one destination to another so that it can be shipped to other countries.

The Spanish introduced wheat to South America in the 1550s. Only one-eighth of South America's land is suitable for farming.

Forestry in South America is dominated by eucalyptus and pinus trees. Both types of trees can be used for timber and wood fiber.

Goods and Services

Many South American countries export their goods to other countries. The United States, Japan, and Europe are South America's main trading partners. Oil and petroleum are two of South America's most important exports.

South America also exports other goods, such as wheat, cattle, and fruit. Countries within the continent trade with each other, too. An organization called the Latin American Integration Association (LAIA), encourages trade between South American countries by reducing the taxes countries pay on traded goods.

Fast Facts

Many countries in South America plan to join Canada, the United States, and Mexico in the North American Free Trade Agreement (NAFTA). This agreement encourages trade between member countries.

Manufacturing is one of the fastest-growing industries in South America. Processed foods, cement, vehicles, and equipment are produced in South America and sold around the world.

Many parts of South America are not as developed as other parts of the world. This means that their industries have not been very strong, and people have suffered through difficult working and living conditions. The countries of South America are working very hard to improve conditions throughout the continent. Many governments encourage people to invest, or put money into, new industries, such as manufacturing. This will improve the economies of many of South America's countries.

More than 70 percent of employees in Brazil work in the service industry, including retail shops and restaurants.

The Past

Indigenous Peoples

South America's earliest inhabitants arrived from North America around 30,000 years ago. Groups, such as the Chibcha, Inca, and Araucanians, settled around the Andes Mountains. Other groups spread out across the plains of central South America. By 1500, about 14 million indigenous peoples lived on the continent.

Fast Facts

People in South America celebrate the Incan festival of *Inti Raymi*, or the Festival of the Sun.

In many parts of Peru, people still speak *Quechua*, the language of the Inca.

Nearly five million of South America's early inhabitants were Inca. The Incan Empire stretched from Chile to Ecuador. Many Incan settlements were high in the mountains. The Incas used advanced technologies, including plumbing and irrigation systems. When the Spanish arrived in South America in the 1500s, they discovered the Incan settlements, including **temples** and statues decorated with silver and gold. Silver and gold were very valuable in Europe, so the Spanish attacked the Incan settlements, stole their riches, and killed many people. They claimed the land for Spain and forced many Incas to work in mines as **slaves**.

Today, there are about 26 million indigenous peoples in South America. Groups such as the Yanomami still live a traditional lifestyle. There are about 16,000 Yanomami living in Brazil.

This illustration from the early 1890s shows Spanish missionary Vicente de Valverde teaching Christianity to Incan emperor Atahualpa.

The Age of Exploration

Christopher Columbus, an Italian explorer who sailed on behalf of Spain, was the first European to reach South America's shores. He landed in Venezuela. In 1499, Amerigo Vespucci also landed in Venezuela. Vespucci traveled east until he reached the Amazon River.

Other Spanish explorers traveled to South America in the 1500s. Pedro Alvares Cabral claimed present-day Brazil for Portugal. The Spanish **conquered** large parts of South America, including the Incan Empire in 1532.

By the end of the 1500s, Portugal controlled most of southeast South America, and Spain controlled the rest of the continent. Conquerors from France, Great Britain, and Holland arrived in the 1600s and claimed small territories on South America's northeast coast.

Christopher Columbus reached South America when sailing west across the Atlantic Ocean in search of a route to Asia.

Fast Facts

Amerigo Vespucci explored the northern coast of South America in 1499 and 1500.

The Magellan Strait separates Cape Horn from the island of Tierra del Fuego. The strait was named after Ferdinand Magellan, who discovered the body of water while exploring the island in 1520.

Pedro Alvares Cabral was a conquistador. Conquistador was the name given to Spanish explorers who conquered parts of North and South America in the 1500s.

Early Settlers

Europeans established settlements around the mines and plantations in South America. Slaves worked in the mines and on the plantation fields. The first slaves were indigenous South Americans who had been captured by Europeans. The Europeans brought diseases that killed many South Americans. Poor living conditions caused others to become ill and die. When there were no longer enough indigenous South Americans to work as slaves, the Europeans brought Africans to South America. Ports along the coasts shipped the goods produced in South America to Europe. Cities, such as Buenos Aires and Rio de Janeiro, grew around these ports.

This engraving from 1750 shows an overseer sitting in the shade while workers harvest coffee beans.

Most South Americans have European **ancestors**. This is because Spain, Portugal, France, Holland, and England invaded South America in the 1500s and divided its territories. The cultures of the people who settled South America blended with the traditions of the indigenous South Americans to create the cultures and traditions people across the continent share today.

By the 1700s, many South Americans were unhappy with Spanish and Portuguese rule. People had to pay high taxes. **Rebellions** broke out because South Americans wanted control over their land. Between 1810 and 1816, Argentina, Paraguay, and Uruguay fought for their independence from Spain. A series of other wars were fought between 1816 and 1825, until all of the colonies won their independence.

Fast Facts

Many revolutionaries, or leaders who supported South American independence, are considered heroes. Leaders, such as Simón Bolívar, Francisco de Miranda, and José de San Martín, are celebrated for their achievements.

Brazil declared independence from Portugal in 1822, but kept its ties to the country's monarch, or leader, until 1889.

Che Guevara was an Argentine doctor who fought for the independence of many Latin American countries. Many people consider him a hero.

The wars fought between 1810 and 1825 are known as the "Wars of Independence."

People celebrate Simón Bolívar because he helped to free Venezuela, Colombia, Peru, Ecuador, and Bolivia from Spanish rule. Bolivia was named in his honor. Bolívar wrote Bolivia's constitution in 1826.

Culture

Population

More than 360 million people live in South America. The small continent is one of the most populated places on Earth. Most South Americans live in coastal cities, such as Buenos Aires in Argentina, Montevideo in Uruguay, and Caracas in Venezuela. Nearly 50 percent of South America's population lives in Brazil.

Most South Americans are of Spanish, Portuguese, African, or Native-American descent. People from Argentina, Brazil, and Uruguay also descend from Italians, Germans, and **Poles**. Some descendants of nineteenth-century Chinese **immigrants** live in Guyana. Many Japanese people live in Brazil, Bolivia, and Paraguay.

In South America, most people speak Spanish, but many also speak Portuguese. Some people still speak their native languages, including *Quechua*, a language used by the ancient Incans.

Fast Facts

Bolivia has the largest population of indigenous South Americans. Sixty percent of Bolivians claim to be descended from South America's earliest inhabitants.

South America is home to 6 percent of the world's total population.

The population of South America grows by 2.4 percent each year.

Mestizo is the name given to people who are of both Spanish and Native-American descent. In Brazil, these people call themselves *Mestico*.

Nearly 12 percent of South Americans claim African descent. Many South Americans of African descent are Yoruban. The Yoruban culture influences everything from music to festivals in South America.

About 6 million people live in Rio de Janeiro.

Politics and Government

Since the countries of South America gained their independence from Spain, Portugal, France, Holland, and Great Britain, they have faced other struggles.

Until the 1990s, dictators ruled many South American countries. Dictators are leaders who have the complete power to make decisions, regardless of what the people of the country want. Today, South American countries hold democratic elections. A democracy is a form of government in which the people of the country vote for their leaders and are able to voice their opinion if they do not like the decisions their leaders make.

Fast Facts

A president rules most South American countries. Guyana is the only country with a prime minister. The prime minister traditionally reported to Great Britain's king or queen. Countries with ties to Great Britain, such as Canada, have prime ministers.

In Bolivia, the president leads for 4 years, which is called a term. It is illegal for a president to run for election two terms in a row.

In Brazil, people between the ages of 18 and 70 must vote, or they can be punished by law.

Montevideo is the capital of Uruguay. Montevideo's congress is housed in a marble building.

Cultural Groups

South Americans share many different traditions, including languages, religions, and celebrations. Many of their traditions are unique. Indigenous South Americans are fighting to keep their languages and traditions alive. Some people hold special classes so that they can teach children how to speak, read, and write in their native languages. They also teach their religious beliefs and cultural traditions.

Most South Americans speak Spanish. In Brazil, most people speak Portuguese, the country's official language. In other parts of South America, people also speak Dutch and French. Native languages, including Quechua, Aymara, and Guaraní, are also spoken in the west, and in Bolivia, Chile, and Peru.

Roman Catholicism, a Christian religion, is the main religion practiced in South America. Jewish people live throughout South America, especially in the cities of Argentina and Brazil. In Guyana and Suriname, Hindus, Buddhists, and Muslims worship at temples and mosques.

A 100-foot (30-meter) tall statue of Christ the Redeemer stands on a 20-foot (6-meter) pedestal on the peak of Corcovado Mountain in Rio de Janeiro.

Religious celebrations are popular in South America. Many Christians celebrate Christmas and Easter. People also celebrate Hannukah, which is a Jewish celebration, Eid, a Muslim celebration, and Diwali, which is the Hindu festival of light. Other celebrations reflect the cultural backgrounds, beliefs, and communities of the people of South America. *Semana Santa*, *Fiesta de la Virgen de la Candelabria*, and *Dia de la Raza* combine indigenous South American, Spanish, and African traditions.

One of the most widely celebrated South-American festivals is Carnaval. During Carnaval, South America's largest celebration, people dress in colorful masks similar to those made for thanksgiving festivals by their indigenous South American and African ancestors. Cities such as Rio de Janeiro are well known for their Carnaval celebrations. For 4 days, people dance through the streets dressed in colorful costumes. Parades feature brightly painted floats. Many stores, restaurants, and businesses are closed so that everyone can join in the fun. The celebration takes place before **Lent**, one of the most important Christian holidays.

Fast Facts

Spanish is the official language of nine countries in South America.

Nearly 10 million people in Latin America speak Quechua.

About 90 percent of South Americans are Roman Catholic.

The Venezuelan Devil Dancers of Yare Celebration takes place on Corpus Christy Days on May 26 and 27 each year.

Carnaval is Rio de Janeiro's main event. It takes place every summer.

Arts and Entertainment

The cultures, traditions, and histories South Americans share influence their art, music, and films. Some art hangs in world-famous galleries, such as the Mueso de Arte Moderna. The gallery, located in Rio de Janeiro, contains paintings and sculptures by South American and international artists.

Not all art hangs in galleries and museums. In the colorful neighborhood of La Boca, Buenos Aires, many of the buildings are painted with vibrant murals. Others are painted with bright red, blue, yellow, pink, and green paint. The idea came from Quinquela Martín, an artist who used bright colors to paint his Buenos Aires home.

Gabriel García Márquez is a Colombian novelist, short-story writer, and journalist.

Brightly painted wooden houses line some streets in La Boca, located at the mouth of the Riachuelo River in Buenos Aires.

The strong beats, fast rhythms, and beautiful music of South America have influenced many famous singers. Shakira, who was born in Brazil, sings in both English and Spanish. Christina Aguilera was born in the United States to an Ecuadoran father.

Literature from South America is read and celebrated around the world. Some of the best-known authors call South America their home. Colombian author Gabriel García Márquez wrote about the history and lives of his people in his novel *One Hundred Years of Solitude.* Many South-American authors, including Márquez and poet Pablo Neruda, have won the Nobel Prize for Literature. Nobel Prizes are awarded to people who make a valuable contribution to literature, economics, world peace, chemistry, physics, medicine, or psychology.

Fast Facts

Roberto Matta, a well-known painter, was born in Chile. He studied a style of art called surrealism in Paris. Surrealist painters use bright shapes and blurry objects to depict scenes in daily life and nature.

Brazilian director Fernando Meirelle was nominated for an Academy Award in 2004 for his movie *City of God.*

Shakira wrote her first song when she was 8 years old. She signed her first recording contract at age 13.

Sports

From skiing snowy mountain peaks to exploring humid rain forests and swimming in sparkling waters, the people of South America love to participate in sports and other activities. Hiking, swimming, snorkeling, and playing sports are just some of the ways people in South America pass their time.

In South America, soccer is called football. Football is the most popular sport in South America. People in all South American countries enjoy this sport, which is played by two teams of eleven players. The object of the game is to score goals by kicking the ball into the other team's net. South America is known for its skilled soccer players, which include Diego Maradona, Ronaldo, and Edson Arantes do Nascimento, better known as Pelé.

Millions of South Americans eagerly watch the World Cup soccer championships, which are held every 4 years. During each championship there are two tournaments, one for women and one for men. Brazil has won the World Cup five times.

Fast Facts

Basketball is also a popular sport in South America. Players dribble, or bounce, a ball across a court and try to throw it through their opponents' net.

In South America, football is spelled *futbol*.

European sailors introduced football to South Americans in the 1800s. They played the game in Buenos Aires, Argentina.

Race-car driving is popular in South America, especially in Brazil. Ayrton Senna and Emerson Fittipaldi are two well-known Brazilian race-car drivers. Both drivers have won many championship races, including the World Grand Prix Formula One race, which is a competition held between drivers from around the world.

Ayrton Senna died in 1994 during the San Marino Grand Prix race. He crashed into a concrete wall while driving at a speed of 186 miles (300 km) per hour.

Brain Teasers

1. What group of people lived in cities that now stand in ruin in the Andes Mountains?

2. Which three bodies of water surround South America?

3. How many countries are in South America? What are their names?

4. What is the nickname given to the Andes Mountains?

5. Where do guanacos and vicuñas live?

6 What are empanadas?

7 Where does rubber come from?

8 How many Inca lived in South America when the Spanish arrived?

9 What are plantations? What crops were grown on plantations?

10 Which South American country has the highest population?

ANSWER KEY

1. the Inca
2. the Caribbean Sea, in the north; the Atlantic Ocean in the east; and the Pacific Ocean in the west
3. twelve; Argentina, Bolivia, Brazil, Chile, Colombia, Ecuador, Guyana, Paraguay, Peru, Suriname, Uruguay, and Venezuela. French Guiana, located in the northeast, is owned by France.
4. the backbone of South America
5. the Andes Mountains
6. pastries filled with meat, vegetables, seafood, cheese, or fruit
7. rubber trees
8. 5 million
9. large farms; sugarcane, coffee, and tobacco
10. Brazil

For More Information

Books

Check the school or public library for more information about South America. The following books have useful information about the continent:

Bright, Michael. *BBC/Animal Planet: South America Revealed*. New York: Dorling Kindersley Publishing; 1st edition, 2001.

Burger, Richard and Lucy Salazar. *Machu Picchu: Unveiling the Mysteries of the Inca*. New Haven, CT: Yale University Press, 2004.

Minnis, Natalie. *Insight Guide South America.* Washington, D. C.: APA Publications; 4th edition, 2002.

Web sites

You can also go online and have a look at the following Web sites:

South America Tourism Office
www.southamericatourism.com

CIA World Factbook
www.cia.gov/cia/publications/factbook

South American Explorers
www.saexplorers.org

Ecuador Explorer
www.ecuadorexplorer.com

Brazil Tourism
www.embratur.gov.br/en/home/index.asp

Glossary

ancestors the people from whom an individual is descended

conquered taken over by force

equator an imaginary line drawn around the center of Earth that separates the Northern Hemisphere from the Southern Hemisphere, or two halves of the globe

eroded worn away over time by wind or water

exported sent to another country to sell

fertile able to support plants and crops well

glaciers large, slow-moving masses of ice

habitats the environments in which plants or animals live

historians people who study history

immigrants people who move from one country to live in another

Inca people who lived in the Andes Mountains during the fifteenth century

indigenous the first people living in a particular country or region

Lent the 40 days before Easter

minerals substances formed in the earth that are not of plants or animals

Poles people from Poland

rebellions uprisings; armed fights against the government or people who make rules

salsa a musical style that blends Cuban rhythms with jazz, rock, and soul music

slaves people who are forced to work for other people against their will

temples houses of worship

Index